Sun Hats & Staying Home

To my dear husband David, family, and friends who enrich my travels and my staying at home. A special thanks to Doro, who both helped design the front cover and has been unfailingly supportive in my poetry writing.

Sun Hats & Staying Home

Wendy Westley

BREWIN BOOKS

BREWIN BOOKS
19 Enfield Ind. Estate,
Redditch,
Worcestershire,
B97 6BY
www.brewinbooks.com

Published by Brewin Books 2025

© Wendy Westley 2025

The author has asserted her rights in accordance with the Copyright, Designs and Patents Act 1988 to be identified as the author of this work.

All rights reserved. No part of this publication may be reproduced, stored in a retrieval system, or transmitted in any form or by any means, electronic, mechanical, photocopying, recording or otherwise, without the prior permission in writing of the publisher and the copyright owners, or as expressly permitted by law, or under terms agreed with the appropriate reprographics rights organization. Enquiries concerning reproduction outside the terms stated here should be sent to the publishers at the UK address printed on this page.

A CIP catalogue record for this book is available from the British Library.

ISBN: 978-1-85858-780-6

Printed and bound in Great Britain
by 4edge Ltd.

Contents

Introduction 7

The Sun Hat 8

Flight 603, an Unforgettable Flight 10

I Didn't Travel Far Today 15

My Coral Necklace (I am a Murderer) 17

Palmyra 20

Biscuit Tins and Desert Storms 21

The Name Dropper 26

A Frog in a Box 28

Tangerines and Handkerchiefs on a Kibbutz Sabbath 32

Labels 34

Home 36

I Love my Home... Wendy writes 39

Introduction

Sun Hats & Staying Home is a collection of poetry and stories about holidays, people, and living hopefully.

Sometimes Wendy feels she has been a traveller all her life, even though there have been times she hasn't travelled far at all.

Wendy has had a successful and varied career as a nurse, midwife, counsellor, therapist, and volunteer.

She is a Christian poet, pilgrim and good friend. She hopes you enjoy her work, whether on holiday or at home, with a cup of coffee (or even wine).

The Sun Hat

If one plus one makes two,
I wonder if my packing plus the holiday
Makes the stress worthwhile.
My packing starts months ahead and takes up
The spare room, despite my husband's groans.
My travel boxes are full of essentials
Like mosquito stuff and chargers for the phone,
Plasters and medication,
My Blenheim Palace sun hat, my crowning glory.

I bought this hat on impulse
At B.P. when the snow fell and other people
Drank hot toddies and mulled wine,

And I dreamt of glamour, sunshine and golden sands.
It is cream and bendy, it folds in half,
I can put it in my bag or in my case
Or on my head, and I feel like a princess.

My impulse buy sits in my holiday box
And when I see it, cool and fresh,
It's as if it hasn't seen me hot and sweaty in the sun
Or sipping cocktails before midday.
I am full of joy
That I'm on my holidays.
It holds memories of trips abroad, and even
Back at home where (unlikely though it seems)
The sun does shine.

The packing is, of course, always stressful,
And clothes are brought in and out,
Along with trainers, sandals and even boots.
It shouldn't really matter, of course,
Because the locals are invariably kind and
Will never meet me again.
They probably won't remember
If the colours matched,
If I looked fat or thin.
It really doesn't matter what I pack
As long as I have my sun hat. ∎

Flight 603, an Unforgettable Flight

Despite being a frequent flyer for work, I never really got over my deep anxiety of flying. I'd been anxious all my life but I had taken some self-help courses on stress management and public speaking that had helped, so I was getting better at hiding my vulnerability. I had booked my favourite hotel for the night, knowing that I would be able to deal with the important business meeting, and be home by tomorrow night. Flight 603 was just something to be endured, like all flights.

Nevertheless, I was pleased to be sat next to a really nice man, Robert, who took my mind off the flight by sharing his own fears. He was going on a business trip too, leaving his poorly partner Mark at home with some kind and reliable carers, although he was still worried. He'd been a travel agent for far too long, he admitted, and he'd got sick of it. Tedious hours away at the office added to his guilt and anxiety about leaving Mark alone for long periods. I sympathised. I'd looked after my own elderly mother until she had died.

Robert lightened the mood when he confided that he was keen to try this new airline as it promised good value and we wondered what added *'extras'* on Flight 603 would transpire. We had a good laugh guessing what this could be. I wanted some unusual snacks, while Robert hoped for a cocktail. Neither of us were that optimistic!

While we were having complimentary drinks (not cocktails!) and crisps, I was aware of increasing laughter behind us. There were two young people, talking about their plans on arrival, and it was clear they were getting very friendly. I think her name was Suzie and I overheard that she too was fed up with her work as a translator, as working from home did get a bit lonely. She would have liked her language degree to have opened more exciting doors.

The young man, Josh I found out later, was apparently meeting a new girlfriend and he admitted he was very nervous because he was so shy – his relationships were always short-lived. I smiled when I heard Suzie giving him lots of advice and I thought if they drank any more, he might not need to meet a new girlfriend!! They seemed to be getting on famously.

It was just before lunch was served that I started to be aware of a strange noise. It was alarming. I heard Josh reassure Suzie that there was nothing to worry about. He was sitting by the window and all looked ok. I was sitting in an aisle seat and was aware the cabin crew were starting to look anxious. Suddenly there was a huge amount of turbulence and the overhead warning lights flashed red, instructing us to fasten our seat belts. I'm not sure how long the noise and turbulence lasted, but another announcement plunged me into full panic mode. Suddenly, despite all my self-help work, I began to panic. I couldn't breathe and was grabbing poor Robert's hand, when we were then instructed:

'Please put on the oxygen mask that is dropping from overhead. Make sure you put on your mask before you try to assist anyone else.'

More panic erupted, not just mine. I thought my chest was being crushed and I was gasping for breath. My heart was racing and I truly thought we were going to crash. I was aware that I was making more noise than anyone and I felt terrified. Suddenly I was assisted by a wonderful steward, who promised me it would be alright. 'You're Ok, you are doing Ok, I am here to help.' He offered to hold my other hand and started to give me soothing instructions, 'Sigh out slowly. Breathe…'

Some time later, a second bell broke into the noise. 'Apologies everyone. We are pleased to tell you there is absolutely no cause for alarm. Our stewardess has pressed the alarm in error. Please take off your masks. As soon as the turbulence is over, you will be pleased we will be serving lunch.'

I can't really describe everyone's reaction. Relief, anger, nervous laughter. Quite a few expletives. It was only later that we started to admit to each other the thoughts that had been going through all of our minds. Firstly, I apologised profusely, sheepishly explaining I hadn't had a panic attack for years. I was so sorry I'd been such a bother. Josh looked ashen, and assured me it was totally understandable, as he had thought he was going to die. Suzie was very kind and admitted she felt helpless because she hadn't known what to do. 'Wasn't the steward marvellous?' she enthused. We all agreed that we were extremely impressed with the competence of the steward, but Suzie was bowled over. Robert concurred; he was very fearful too. He admitted to me quietly that this *'extra'*, if that's what it was, was the very last straw. Near retirement age, he felt it was a sign, time to wind up his business and actually spend time with his Mark. Feeling this could have been his last moment certainly focused his mind. Life was too short and he wanted to live it to the full while he could.

I reflected it was time to change my way of working too, and also get some professional help. I appreciated the stewardess's error was a rare one, but the panic had been alarming and I didn't ever want a repetition of such terror.

By the end of Flight 603, we four had become very friendly. We discussed it was probably the worst flight we'd ever been on and wouldn't fly with the company again. I reassured everyone I'd get some professional help for my anxiety. Robert said he'd never fly again either, but for more positive reasons: retirement and time with Mark. Josh said he couldn't wait to spend time with his new girlfriend and wasn't going to let his shyness blight this new relationship, as it had in the past. Suzie had chatted to the helpful steward at length, complimenting him on his wonderful handling of the situation, and later announced to us that she would be applying to the airline for a job, as it would not only put her language skills to better use, but it would also be more interesting too.

Certainly Flight 603 was a flight, I suspect, none of us would ever forget. I never worked out what the *'extra'* was, but I can assure you that I have no intention of ever trying the airline again to find out. Also, I have not had a panic attack since. ■

I Didn't Travel Far Today

I didn't travel far today
But walked the roads
To take the air
And flex my legs
And have a nose.

I am a city girl,
So, I spot the drives and newest doors
And see bold designs are in the mix.
But I never thought I'd find the joyous gift
Of a country garden.

I'm such a city girl
I didn't know the names
Or couldn't tell from leaves and shapes
Their origin.
But I loved them all the same.

I don't know all my neighbours,
Just a few,
And I do not know the person
Who designed the plot
With such precision
And care and beauty and love.

One day I hope I can share
My surprise and gratitude,
And be brave enough to ring the bell
To say thank you from a city girl,
For such a tranquil country garden. ■

My Coral Necklace
(I am a Murderer)

I wear a noose around my neck
But I am, in fact, the murderous one.
My beautiful orange-spiked rope
Once held life forms of polyps, mollusc and
Vibrant sea grass.

Corals, they are soldiers battling climate change;
An ecosystem unsurpassed.
Their reefs could even tame tumultuous waves
And bring peace to the far off shore.

Thank God
There are now new warriors
Who try to combat stupidity
Like mine,
Although I was told
All farming is done responsibly.
Now I wonder how.

Coral is also birthed in laboratories,
Nurtured in tanks with moderated light
That speaks of moonbeams.

They speak of cease-fires as
New life arrives to moderate
A dying planet.

On the waves, too,
There are nurseries of net
Where sperm and ova meet
In collecting jars
For hopeful and miraculous IVF,
So, corals that are weak and
Infertile, or in the throes of death
Are replenished.

> The colours of the coral
> Are resplendent,
> Calling out to ignorant and shallow
> Tourists like me.
> Unwitting sirens,
> They are in fact the victims,
> And I am now ashamed.
> The brittle and most beautiful
> Scaffold-armour
> Once held teeming life.

I am, of course, a most unwitting murderer. ∎

Palmyra

Biscuit Tins and Desert Storms

I have so many memories of this country, so full of awesome beauty, that I find it hard to know where to begin. I wonder what it's really like now. I'm almost afraid to ask. There have been so many tragedies.

I was on a tour in Syria, in around 2008, too scared to go alone but not so cowardly that I didn't want to go somewhere different. There were stories of fantastic Roman remains, ancient cities, museums and mosques and I wanted to see Umayyad, the largest and oldest mosque in the world for myself. Like many sites, it holds interest to Christians and Muslims, but there, tradition holds that the head of St. John the Baptist is buried there in a golden shrine.

Unlike Christian churches, there are no representations of God, saints or humanity. All is marble, mosaic and space to worship. The carpets are luxurious and spotlessly clean, as all shoes are left outside.

What has stayed in my memory though, are the peripheral memories: the kaleidoscope of colours, the smell of spices, the generosity of the locals and dear Hussein Hussein, our guide, with his humour and messages from his mother.

Each day there was a different biscuit tin, with different cookies, made in his mother's kitchen each morning. They were delivered with enthusiasm and the widest smile I've ever seen.

My fellow travellers were eclectic, one or two unmemorable. My favourite recollection is of a dear couple of advancing years (well, it seemed to me, as I was still a youngster). Both artists, with camera and basket of pencils and watercolours, they enabled me to see Syria through their filters of perspective, shade, colour and wonder.

One wonderful day, filled with the splendour and majesty of Palmyra, we wandered reluctantly back to our transport, when Hussein Hussein yelled loudly, 'Run, run!'

There had been whispers of tensions, and someone cried fearfully, 'Is it the Iraqis?!' However inaccurate the question was, it made us all run faster.

Safely sat in our vehicle, the darkness suddenly descended and we were unable to move. The bombardment was sand; the attack – a desert sandstorm. Sand was seeping into the vehicle and the air was becoming murky. Being asthmatic, I was finding it difficult to breathe. Outside all was silence. We also fell silent and were full of fear and foreboding. I think I prayed. Slowly the bus was able to edge forward, and soon the air was clear again. There was such relief to be on our way; it was a chilling reminder that Nature is never to be underestimated. It was an experience too, that was never adequately captured in paint.

A large part of the trip was visiting other mosques, many of which still held the stillness and peace of a place of worship, but not many were as grand as the one in Damascus. They all felt unworldly, were beautifully designed, geometric, and orderly in form. Inside, the atmosphere was peaceful, calm, and I always felt there was a spirituality there.

Outside was a different matter, as there was often such a crush to get in. Women and men were segregated, and I was given a rather well-used burqa to wear. Dressed all in black from top to toe, I felt I'd been assimilated into a dark mass of anonymity. I felt a bit panicky – would my group ever find me? Never have I been more grateful for my one distinctive feature of that holiday: my red handbag. I'd discovered it was my own personal tracking device. (My BP sun hat came later!)

Being Western travellers, keen to see as much as we could of this fascinating country, we were nevertheless always keen to have lunch! Our travel guide, Hussein Hussein, recognising our Western wimpiness (or as he kindly put it, our lack of

Arabic), suggested that he sorted out our lunchtime food, as we were travelling extensively every day. The cost was always the same – for a main course, a dessert and a drink, even alcohol, it was the equivalent of £2.50. *In for a penny, in for a piastre*, I thought.

Every lunch was delicious. Fresh bread, salads, meat or fish or vegetables. By the last day, we were anticipating yet another rustic lunch when Hussein Hussein announced, 'We have a feast.' We were sceptical, of course, as only Westerners could be. But out came aromatic rice, vegetables, salads, and half a sheep! What would this cost, we all wondered. Hussein Hussein smiled, used to disbelieving foreigners. '£2.50 of course.'

We feasted like kings, drank like fish, and laughed like friends.

We were full, and happy. No need for tins of biscuits today. ■

The Name Dropper

Dripping with jewellery
And skin burned to a crisp,
She recites her itinerary
As though it were a blessing.
She is an acquaintance whose
Travelogue reminds me
Of the glossy magazines
And colour supplements
That label each draped
With designer names.

What about the people who sold the clothes
In crowded shops, with aching feet?
The people who sweated to make them,
Perhaps even little children?

The people who served on the cruise ships
Are often nameless;
In the laundry,
In the kitchens
Washing up.
Corfu, Crete, Spain.
Cunard, Princess.
Glamourous places,
Anonymous people.

I think though of the times
I can't name drop.
The forgotten names of the people
Who changed my sheets,
Who cleaned my room,
Who welcomed me with such warmth,
Whose countries are now at war.
Who no longer are alive
But are remembered,
Although I too can't remember their names. ∎

A Frog in a Box

China was inspiring. Vast and modern, steeped in history and superstitious, it was all I expected and much more. The Great Wall of China was evocative in the mist but largely hidden on the horizon by the horde of tourists.

Buildings were so spectacularly designed and built, sometimes you felt you were on a film set. Hotel restaurants offered every cuisine imaginable, so you could have vegetable soup, egg fried rice and stir fry, egg and bacon or vindaloo for breakfast.

Dynasties came to life – well, almost – as we saw with the Terracotta Warriors in Xi'an, with horses and chariots, weapons and armour, and every figure unique, just like the fighting men they had been.

The toilets in the rural areas were also something else! Stalls featured holes in the ground, with proper surrounds and taps, though one had to be pretty nifty to avoid the flush or you would have wet feet for the remainder of the day. On one of the first days of our tour, our guide escorted all the women to a quiet room for a 'crouching tiger, hidden dragon' lesson. We were taught how to hitch our skirts or trouser legs up, perfect our kneeling, hold our balance and… You can then imagine afterwards, one had to reverse the procedure with no mishaps. Well, that was the plan. So, the toilets were not going to be a surprise, until of course they were.

Entering one block, I was faced with a number of crouching tigers, so to speak, with doors wide open. I found out most locals thought opening and shutting the doors was most unhygienic. (Think about how many hands would touch the handles.) A further surprise was that there was always running water, soap and hand gel. Better equipped than in some toilets at home, I think.

Bicycles were another surprise. Hundreds of them. Not every family could afford a car, and it was awe-inspiring to see whole families on one bike with the weekly shop. Car drivers seemed to have the knack of manoeuvring at high speed through equally speeding oncoming traffic, without a scratch.

Although I didn't see any road accidents, our cruise along the Three Gorges came to an abrupt end after our Captain crashed our ship, which was duly abandoned. But we had enjoyed wonderful scenery and spectacular locks, and the Three Gorges Dam really was an engineering wonder. The tour was hastily rearranged and we took many local flights, thus seeing cities, museums and local highlights that were never in our itinerary.

On the main holiday, we celebrated joyfully along with Chinese families, all dressed up and picnicking – the highlight of the trip being the family of pandas at the zoo in Chongqing. Such were the crowds that, despite our towering size, we thought we would never get a glimpse. The locals, however, were super proud of their pandas, and – being unfailingly polite and courteous – allowed us to get to the front. We were truly honoured guests.

The local flights were less orderly, as well as turbulent, and we were told in-flight meals were more like snacks – perhaps 'A Frog in a Box' according to our tour guide. (I don't think it was a joke.) We'd had unusual meals and beverages before, such as snake wine, which was meant to be an aphrodisiac, deep-fried bee larvae, and Century eggs, although I don't think anything was that old. In fact, the contents of the box were unmemorable.

Our proficiency at eating with chopsticks increased with each meal. We even ate with the locals in the street markets, where aromatic and colourful food was cooked fresh, over sizzling flames. Our enjoyment was diminished only by the local 'paparazzi' who kept taking our photos sideways on, because they were fascinated by our 'big noses'.

Of course, my stories reflect my uncultured ignorance as I'm always more impressed by the people I see and meet than the famous buildings or historical facts. I will never forget the welcome and the joy on the local villagers' faces when I joined them in their daily park exercises: Tai Chi. A more gentle and serious form of 'crouching tiger, hidden dragon', perhaps. ■

Tangerines and Handkerchiefs on a Kibbutz Sabbath

Following the Law in the Bible
Was never meant to be a trial.
And the Rabbis (like all
Men of God, I'm told).
Were only trying to be helpful
(But there's always such a lot about
Punishment and stoning).

But how could the picking of a
Juicy, succulent tangerine
On a hot and dusty
Galilean Holy day be such a terrible sin?
(There's also a lot about feeding).

The handkerchief was another thing
Stitched to Sabbath clothing.
Perhaps it is different now,
Since the arrival of Covid,
When you must blow your nose
And disinfect your hands?
(There's a lot, of course, about purity.)

The family themselves
Were so welcoming, to their Gentile guests.
They shared their lukewarm food,
Prepared the day before with love,
From huge thermos flasks.
The food was kosher, too.

It struck me, though, as very odd,
To talk about rights and wrongs
And sins
As we talked of God
And the men showed off their guns
As fear was ever there.

At visit's end, our family waved us goodbye
With promises, next time, of tangerines. ∎

Labels

I've made mistakes aplenty
As I've journeyed through my life.
Donned with uniform or apron
Or just a smile, I have had my fill of labels.
I'm unsure if the label 'Christian'
Suits me though, as I've failed a lot
(I think I warned you at the start).
I can't say 'Born Again', or 'Made
Like Christ', whether in christening robe,
Or at my confirmation.
Later, I got baptised in a lonely pool
On a snowy wintry day
To my family's disgust.
I so longed to travel better.

They knew what I did not,
But I know now
That all these things are just
A tiny part.
It's faith and love and light
That shows you what is 'in the tin',
And for those I've hurt on my journey,
As I've tried to be a proper pilgrim,
I offer you my love and
Sincere apology. ■

❤

Home

I love my home, it is a sanctuary,
A safe place when things get too much.
Of course, there is the tyranny of domesticity,
Garden weeds and intermittent post,
That arrives with its never-ending flyers and bills.

I love watching the seasons though,
Through conservatory windows.
From the bedroom we can see our new friend, Mr. Fox,
Surveying his kingdom, next door's garden.
I quietly savour the sun's morning glow,
Before my day begins
With fresh coffee in my hand.

Spring is a joy with flowers emerging
And birds singing their hearts out.
There is the promise of warmer days,
With friends sharing food and wine,
Blessed by sunsets in front of the fire-pit.

There are colours too, that last till autumn.
Though the frost and occasional snow
Shall clothe the sleeping garden
With peace and stark beauty,
But not yet.

As the chill of autumn arrives,
The leaves burnish gold and copper bright.
I retreat indoors,
Tempted out only by Indian summer warmth,
Golden sunsets and my beloved's fire-pit.

I know my travelling will be restricted
By weather, illness, friends, family
And many other pressures,
So, I will welcome the gifts of lit fires,
Candlelight and winter comfort food.

I must swap my Blenheim Palace hat
For a cosy dressing gown and furry slippers.
I will bask in the warmth of a home well built,
Safe from war, protected from violence and starvation,
And be grateful for this sanctuary.

It will also be a place of welcome,
For neighbours, family and dear friends,
And other fellow travellers
Who are far away from home.
There will be sharing, laughter and
Food and drink.
Friendship and authenticity
And more stories to share. ■

I Love my Home... Wendy writes:

Thank you for travelling with me as I write about my thoughts on holidays, people I have met and the things I have done.

Perhaps you may be able to share a coffee and friendship with me, in my lovely home in the UK, where I live with my lovely husband and where my two amazing children grew up.

It is where I rest, plan and write, and hopefully give joy to my friends at home and across the world.

I hope you enjoy this small collection as much as I have enjoyed writing it. ■